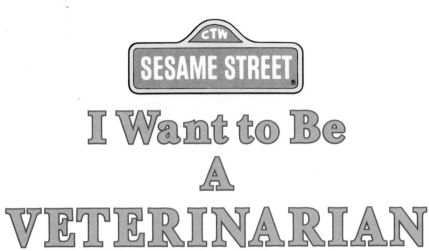

SESAME STREET®

I Want to Be
A
VETERINARIAN

By Michaela Muntean
Illustrated by Tom Cooke

A SESAME STREET/GOLDEN PRESS BOOK
Published by Western Publishing Company, Inc.,
in conjunction with Children's Television Workshop.

© 1992 Children's Television Workshop. Sesame Street puppet characters © 1992 Jim Henson Productions, Inc. All rights reserved. Printed in the U.S.A. No part of this book may be reproduced or copied in any form without written permission from the publisher. Sesame Street and the Sesame Street sign are registered trademarks and service marks of Children's Television Workshop. All other trademarks are the property of Western Publishing Company, Inc. Library of Congress Catalog Card Number: 91-75490   ISBN: 0-307-13116-5/ISBN: 0-307-63116-8 (lib. bdg.)   A   MCMXCII

Today I had to take Barkley to the doctor. Barkley wasn't sick. It was time for his yearly checkup. Animals need to have checkups just like people. Doctors who take care of animals have a special name. They are called veterinarians.

I like to visit the veterinarian with Barkley.

When we arrived, there was a girl with a new puppy
waiting to see Dr. Duberman.
"What's your puppy's name?" I asked.
"Woofer," said the girl.
I said hello to Woofer, and Barkley said hello, too.
"Woof," said Barkley.

"Woof," answered Woofer.

I remember when Barkley was a puppy. The doctor told me how to take care of him. He told me how to bathe Barkley and brush him. He told me what to feed him and how to train him. Teaching people how to take good care of their pets is part of a veterinarian's job.

The doctor called Woofer's name, and he and the girl went into the examining room. While we were waiting, other people and their pets arrived. Some of the animals hadn't come just for a checkup. There was a bird with a hurt wing. There was a cat with a cast on one leg.

The doctor called Barkley's name, and it was our turn to go into the examining room. Barkley wasn't worried. He'd been there before, and Dr. Duberman was kind and gentle.

"Hello, Barkley," said Dr. Duberman as he patted Barkley on the head. "You seem to be just fine, but I want to have a closer look at you."

The veterinarian listened to Barkley's heartbeat with a stethoscope.

He looked in Barkley's eyes and ears with a little flashlight.

He checked his teeth to make sure they were clean and strong. A veterinarian is also an animal's dentist.

The doctor weighed Barkley on a big scale. Then he
checked Barkley's paws and looked at his fur and skin.
"Good," said Dr. Duberman. "No fleas." Next he gave
Barkley his yearly shot. It only hurt for a minute.

When the doctor was finished, he said, "That's all
for today. A fine checkup for a fine, healthy dog."

Barkley said, "Woof," and I said, "Good-bye, Doctor.
Thank you." Then Barkley and I were on our way.

Maybe someday I will be a veterinarian like Dr. Duberman and take care of animals. I know you have to go to school and study very hard. There are lots of things you have to learn to be a veterinarian.

After I graduate from school, I will have an office just like Dr. Duberman's. It will have an X-ray machine so I can see if an animal has any broken bones.

I will carry a flashlight, and I will wear a stethoscope around my neck. When animals are sick, I will give them medicine to make them well.

I will take care of all kinds of pets—cats and dogs
and bunnies and turtles and guinea pigs and
even goldfish.

Some veterinarians take care of farm animals.
Maybe that's what I will do! Then I will have to visit my
patients on the farm, because it is very hard to bring a
cow or a goat to an office.

Veterinarians make sure that chickens stay healthy
so they will lay lots of eggs. They take care of dairy cows
so the cows will produce good milk.

Sometimes veterinarians help to deliver the foal when a mother horse is having a baby.

Some veterinarians take care of zoo animals. Maybe that's what I'll do. I wonder how I would take care of an elephant with an earache!

Or a giraffe with a sore throat!

Someday I will learn how to take care of all kinds of animals, whether they have fur or fins or feathers, paws or claws or hooves, because when I grow up…

I want to be a veterinarian!